Bright ★ Sparks

Thank you for buying this Bright Sparks book.
What happens next?

When you or anyone else buys another Bright Sparks book,
we will give a free book to a less fortunate child somewhere in the world.
We have already donated over 100,000 books.

To find out more, and for fun and games,
visit "Sam Sparks" at . . .

www.thebrightsparks.com

We want to help the world to read.

This is a Bright Sparks book
First published in 2001
Bright Sparks, Queen Street House,
4 Queen Street, BATH BA1 1HE, UK
Copyright © Parragon 2001

Designed by Andrea Newton
Language consultant: Betty Root

Printed in Italy.
ISBN 1-84250-418-5

My Grandpa is Great

Written by Gaby Goldsack

Illustrated by Sara Walker

Bright ☆ Sparks

My grandpa is **great**. He always has lots of time for me, even when he's busy.

I always look forward to going to stay with him for the weekend.

Grandpa is a lot like me.
He enjoys getting lovely and dirty.

I just wish Grandma
felt the same way.

Grandpa is a **brilliant** gardener.
His pumpkins are the biggest I've ever seen.

Well, that was until I saw even bigger ones at the village show. Luckily, Grandpa doesn't mind.

He's a **great** sport!

My grandpa is a **great** fisherman.

But he always forgets the size
of the fish that he caught.
Luckily, I'm there to remind him!

Grandpa knows all about the countryside.
He knows the names of every bird and flower.

He even knows the quickest way to get away from danger! It's amazing how fast he can run.

Grandpa is a **fantastic** dancer.

I love dancing with him, but sometimes it makes me feel a bit dizzy. I don't know where he gets his energy.

Grandpa has lots of cool toys.

Sometimes he even lets me play with them!

Grandpa is very handy in the house.
I can't wait to show Grandma
what he's done to the kitchen!

My grandpa is a **brilliant** cook, too.
He says that when I grow up he'll tell me the
secret of making a really good pizza.

Sometimes Grandpa takes me
to watch a match.

He's the star of the team.

Grandpa tells me all kinds of **amazing** stories. It's hard to believe that he used to be a pirate.

I wish I could have seen his big, red pirate ship.

Sometimes, if I'm really lucky,
Grandpa lets me sleep in his tent.

When he's with me, I'm never afraid.

When it's time to go home,
I wave goodbye to Grandpa.

I expect he's really busy when I'm not there to help. My grandpa is so kind and funny. I love going to Grandpa's because ...

my grandpa is G-R-E-A-T!